Ruby's DinNeRTime

by Paul & Emma Rogers

Dutton Children's Books • New York

Another one for Ruby — with love

Library of Congress Cataloging-in-Publication Data
Rogers, Paul.
Ruby's dinnertime / by Paul and Emma Rogers.—1st ed.
p.   cm.
Summary: Although Ruby has enjoyed eating bananas and playing with spaghetti at her baby table,
she now wants to sit at her parents' dining table and eat with a grown-up plate and cup.
ISBN 0-525-46847-1
[1. Dinners and dining—Fiction. 2. Growth—Fiction. 3. Toddlers—Fiction. 4. Stories in rhyme.]
I. Rogers, Emma, ill. II. Title.
PZ8.3.R643 Ru 2002
[E]—dc21 2001047146

Published in the United States 2002 by Dutton Children's Books,
a division of Penguin Putnam Books for Young Readers
345 Hudson Street, New York, New York 10014
www.penguinputnam.com

Originally published in Great Britain 2001 by Orchard Books, London
Typography by Jason Henry
Printed in Singapore
First American Edition   10 9 8 7 6 5 4 3 2 1

Ruby's got a special chair

with a table
of its own.

When she eats, she looks just like a queen upon her throne.

Ruby likes bananas,

and ice cream's
such a treat.

She simply loves spaghetti—
to play with, not to eat!

Ruby's got a special cup.

It's got a
little spout,

so when you shake it in the air,
not all of it comes out.

She's got a
special bowl as well
that sticks onto the tray.

You have to tug
it really hard

before
it comes
away.

She's even got a fork and spoon —

just right for playing her drum.

"Dinnertime!" calls Mommy,

but Ruby doesn't come.

She sometimes
takes an apple

and cookies from the shelf.

She pretends to have a picnic

and eats it all herself.

But Ruby's not
been playing at
picnicking today.

Daddy goes to
bring her in.

Ruby runs away!

"Not come in!"
shouts Ruby.

"Want you to stay
out there!"

Daddy carries Ruby in and sits her on the chair.

Mommy picks the spoon up
and scoops some carrot on.

She lifts the spoon to Ruby's mouth—
but Ruby's mouth has gone.

"Come on now,"
says Mommy.
"Try to eat
some more."

"Ruby finished!"
Ruby says, and
flings it on the
floor.

"Dear, oh dear," says Daddy.
"What's all this about?

Eat up now —
like rabbit."

Ruby spits it out!

Ruby tugs her bib off.
She pulls her chair away.

Whatever is she up to?
Ruby doesn't say.

She goes to get
a cushion,

a grown-up plate and cup.

"Have dinner now!"
says Ruby,

and she eats it all right up!